Magic Ponies

A Special Wish

To Champion, wonderful and steadfast—SB

GROSSET & DUNLAP
Published by the Penguin Group
Penguin Group (USA) Inc., 375 Hudson Street, New York, New York 10014, USA
Penguin Group (Canada), 90 Eglinton Avenue East, Suite 700, Toronto, Ontario M4P 2Y3, Canada
(a division of Pearson Penguin Canada Inc.)
Penguin Books Ltd, 80 Strand, London WC2R 0RL, England
Penguin Ireland, 25 St Stephen's Green, Dublin 2, Ireland (a division of Penguin Books Ltd)
Penguin Group (Australia), 707 Collins Street, Melbourne, Victoria 3008, Australia
(a division of Pearson Australia Group Pty Ltd)
Penguin Books India Pvt Ltd, 11 Community Centre, Panchsheel Park, New Delhi—110 017, India
Penguin Group (NZ), 67 Apollo Drive, Rosedale, Auckland 0632, New Zealand
(a division of Pearson New Zealand Ltd)
Penguin Books, Rosebank Office Park, 181 Jan Smuts Avenue, Parktown North 2193, South Africa
Penguin China, B7 Jaiming Center, 27 East Third Ring Road North,
Chaoyang District, Beijing 100020, China

Penguin Books Ltd., Registered Offices: 80 Strand, London WC2R 0RL, England

Text copyright © 2009 Sue Bentley. Illustrations copyright © 2009 Angela Swan. Cover illustration © 2009 Andrew Farley. First printed in Great Britain in 2009 by Penguin Books Ltd. First published in the United States in 2013 by Grosset & Dunlap, a division of Penguin Young Readers Group, 345 Hudson Street, New York, New York 10014. Grosset & Dunlap is a trademark of Penguin Group (USA) Inc. Printed in the U.S.A.

Library of Congress Cataloging-in-Publication Data is available.

ISBN 978-0-448-46206-6   10 9 8 7 6 5 4 3 2 1

Magic Ponies

A Special Wish

by SUE BENTLEY

illustrated by Angela Swan

Grosset & Dunlap
An Imprint of Penguin Group (USA) Inc.

Prologue

Comet tried to squash a small flutter of hope as he flew back toward his magical island home. "Destiny must be home safely by now!" the young magic pony cried. His twin sister had been lost for a long time.

Spreading his gold-feathered wings, he soared downward, speeding across the wide sea and galloping over the crests of the waves. Soon, Rainbow Mist Island came into view. Its mountains and forests were almost hidden in softly shimmering, multicolored clouds that gave the island its name. Comet's heart lifted. It felt good to be home.

The magic pony drifted over the shore. Rainbow droplets gleamed like jewels on his cream coat and flowing golden mane and tail. Moments later, he touched down onto the grass of a small clearing.

Tossing his head, Comet looked about warily at the huge trees that grew all around, their glowing leaves tinkling faintly. He could feel no trace of the dark horses who wanted to steal his magic.

As the magic pony snorted with satisfaction, there was a movement and an older horse with a wise expression stepped forward.

"Blaze!" Comet bent his neck in a bow before the leader of the Lightning Herd. Blaze's dark eyes softened with affection.

"I am pleased to see you again, Comet. But where is Destiny?" he asked in a deep gentle voice.

"She is not here? Then she is still in danger!" Comet whinnied sadly.

Destiny had playfully borrowed the Stone of Power, which protected the Lightning Herd from the dark horses, but the stone was accidentally lost while the twin magic ponies were playing cloud-chase. Comet later found the stone, but before he could tell Destiny, she ran away, thinking she was in lots of trouble.

"My sister still thinks she has put the Lightning Herd in danger and cannot forgive herself," Comet explained to the older horse. A lump rose in his throat as he realized that his twin sister was alone and in hiding far from home.

Blaze shook his wise old head slowly. "You must go after her again, my young friend. Find Destiny and tell her that the Stone of Power is safe and bring her home."

Comet's deep-violet eyes flashed. He lifted his head. "I will leave at once!"

"Wait!" Blaze ordered. Stamping his foot, he pawed at the grass. A fiery opal, swirling with flashes of rainbow light appeared. "The stone will help you find her."

The magic pony drew closer to the Stone of Power. A tremor passed over his pale silky coat as he peered deeply into the rainbow depths. The stone grew larger and rays of dazzling light spread outward.

An image formed in the center. Comet gasped as he saw Destiny galloping across a green hillside beneath an open blue sky, in a world far away.

"I have to find her!" he whinnied.

There was a bright flash of dazzling violet light, and rainbow mist surrounded Comet. The cream-colored pony, with his flowing golden mane and tail, and gleaming gold-feathered wings, disappeared. In his place there stood an elegant Connemara pony with a dapple-gray coat, a darker gray mane and tail, and glowing deep-violet eyes.

"There is no time to lose. Go now," Blaze urged. "Use this disguise. Find your twin sister and return with her safely."

"I will!" Comet vowed.

The dapple-gray pony's coat ignited with violet sparks. Comet snorted as he felt the power building inside him. The shimmering rainbow mist swirled faster and faster and drew Comet in . . .

Chapter ONE

Marcie Locket felt her heart beat faster as she stood in her garden, looking over the fence into the adjoining field. There was a big old shed on one side— perfect for a stable and storeroom. Her new pony was going to love its paddock!

Marcie beamed as she imagined all the fun she would have looking after a pony of her own. It was going to be wonderful to go out riding whenever she liked. She might even get her dad to help her put a jumping course up in the field.

"Marcie! Where are you?" her mom called impatiently. "We need to go. I'll be waiting for you in the car."

"Coming!" Marcie answered.

Whirling round, she headed up the garden and into the house. The front door slammed shut behind her as she hurried out to the front drive.

"Sorry, Mom!" Bouncing into the front seat, Marcie dumped her school bag on the floor and fastened her seat belt.

"Hmm. I don't need three guesses to know where you've been," Mrs. Locket said, smiling sideways at her as she waited for a gap in the traffic before pulling out. Marcie smiled back, her eyes glowing

with happiness. "When's Dad going to hear about his job promotion?" she asked. He had promised that Marcie could get her pony once his new job was confirmed.

"I think he should find out by the end of the day," her mom replied.

"Great! We can start looking at ponies for sale. It's Friday today, so we've got the whole weekend," Marcie said excitedly.

But then she sighed as she thought about her best friend who had recently moved away. "I wish Lara was still here. She had tons of pony magazines. We could have looked through them to help me decide what kind of pony I should get."

"You really miss her, don't you? It's a shame she had to move so far away. But you both promised to keep in touch by phone and e-mail, didn't you? And Lara can always come to visit during vacations," Mrs. Locket added.

Marcie knew her mom was right, but at that moment it didn't make her feel much better. It wasn't going to be the same without her best friend living around the corner. Marcie and Lara had known each other since they were in preschool and had always been together as they moved up grades. They used to spend every weekend together, taking turns riding Lara's pony, Tramp.

"Lara's going to forget all about me," Marcie said glumly. "She'll be busy making new friends and riding ponies with them."

"I'm sure she'll remember her old friends, too," her mom chided gently. "And don't forget, there'll be a brand-new reason why Lara will be delighted to come and visit."

"Oh yeah! My new pony!" Marcie exclaimed, starting to cheer up a bit again. "Lara will want to know everything about it, and she'll be dying to ride it."

As they drove through the busy streets, Marcie let her thoughts wander, picturing ponies of every breed and color imaginable. There were so many gorgeous ones out there. Where would they buy hers from? What was she going to call him or her?

They reached the school, and Mom dropped her at the entrance. Marcie gave her a kiss and waved as she drove away. Marcie wandered into school in a daze—all she could think about was her new pony!

When she got to her usual desk by the window, she found Jessica Evans already sitting there. Jessica looked up and smiled as Marcie sat down. "Hi, Marcie. Miss Slater told me to sit here. I'm your new desk-buddy!"

Marcie smiled. "Um . . . hi, Jessica. Fine by me." She didn't mind Jessica at all, but no one could ever replace Lara.

As the rest of the class filed in and took their seats, Jessica began telling Marcie about the new computer game she'd gotten for her birthday.

"It's got an amazing console. I was playing games with my brother all last night and I got a really high score! He was really jealous. What did you do?" she asked.

"I put a bits 'n' bridles poster up in my bedroom. It has all the different types, like snaffle bits and flash nosebands," Marcie began enthusiastically. "I'm getting a pony of my own really soon, so I'm thinking about getting new equipment for it . . ." She stopped as she noticed a glazed expression settle on Jessica's face.

"I just don't get ponies and riding at all," Jessica commented. "I mean, what's the big deal about galloping through muddy fields and stuff and being freezing? Then you have to get up early to clean out smelly, old, messy stables and build muck piles, don't you?"

"Well, yes," Marcie admitted. "But I like the smell of horses, and there's other stuff to do that's lots of fun. It's all part of looking after your pony."

Jessica widened her eyes incredulously. "Fun? I'd rather hang upside down in

Jell-O. I'll stick to my computer games, thanks."

"Okay." Marcie didn't know quite what else to say. A small wave of loneliness washed over her and she realized that she was missing Lara more than ever.

The rest of the day seemed to drag on forever and Marcie was relieved when the bell rang for the end of school. The moment Miss Slater dismissed the class, Marcie grabbed her school bag and raced outside to meet her mom.

"Did Dad text you?" she asked eagerly as they drove home.

Mrs. Locket shook her head. "There's no news yet. You'll have to be patient for once. Although I know that's not your strong point!" she said, laughing.

Marcie grinned. "Impatient? Me?!"
When they got home, Marcie ran upstairs
to change out of her school clothes. She
was just putting on her jeans when she
heard the front door. Her dad was home!
Dashing out of her room, she shot back
down the stairs, two steps at a time.

"Hi, Dad!" Marcie sang, looking up
at him excitedly. She stopped; why did
he have such a serious look on his face?
Today was a good day for all of them!

"Hello, sweetie." Mr. Locket hung
up his jacket and then ran his fingers
through his short brown hair. "Where's
your mom?"

"Um . . . in the kitchen making
dinner, I think," Marcie said, starting to
feel like something was wrong.

She went and stood next to her mom

as her dad sat down at the table and began speaking. "I'm afraid I have bad news. We were all called into a meeting late this afternoon and told that the company's closing down," he explained. "I'm going to have to find another job. And to be honest, the way things are right now, that could take some time."

"Oh dear. That's quite a shock." Mrs. Locket sank into a kitchen chair next to her husband and took his hand. "Well, we'll manage. We'll just have to make cutbacks," she decided firmly.

Marcie's heart sank. Something as expensive as a pony would definitely be one of the cutbacks her mom was talking about. But she bit her lip as she looked at Dad. He seemed pale and tense, although he was trying hard to put on a brave face.

She felt really bad for him.

Marcie went and gave both of her parents a hug. "I'm really sorry about your job, Dad. And I can wait a bit longer for my pony."

"Thanks, honey. That's my grown-up girl." Her dad hugged her back and dropped a kiss on the top of her head. "And don't you worry. You mom and I will work this out."

Marcie nodded. She could tell that they had lots to talk about. "I think I'll . . . um . . . go and sit in the garden . . . or something," she said.

Her mom nodded absently.

Marcie went outside and trudged down to the paddock. She sighed as she thought that it could be empty for quite a while. If only Lara was here. Marcie could

have gone over to her house for a long,
comforting talk.

Suddenly, there was movement over
near the old shed.

Marcie's eyes widened in surprise as
a dapple-gray pony with a darker gray

mane and tail appeared from behind it
and began walking toward her.

"Can you help me, please?" it asked in
a velvety neigh.

Chapter
TWO

"Oh!" Marcie did a double take.

She swallowed hard as she gazed at
the pony in utter astonishment. What was
going on? Had her mom and dad bought
it as a surprise?

But how could they have done that,
when her dad had just lost his job?

Marcie couldn't figure out why there
was a pony in her paddock. And her

imagination was obviously working
overtime, because she'd just imagined
that it had spoken to her!

As the pony leaned forward, Marcie
reached a hand toward it. It had a short
elegant head with a slightly dished nose
and unusually large eyes. They were a
stunning deep-violet color and shone
like amethysts.

She had never seen or heard of any
pony with eyes like that before.

"Hello," she breathed softly, letting
it snuffle her to get her scent. "You're
absolutely gorgeous. You look like a
Connemara pony. But how did you get in
here?"

"I have just arrived from far away. My
name is Comet of the Lightning Herd.
What is yours?" asked the pony.

Marcie dropped her hand in shock
and took two steps backward. This
pony really *had* just spoken to her. This
couldn't be happening! Talking ponies
only existed in fairy tales!

But the beautiful pony twitched his
ears forward and stood looking at her
calmly as if waiting for a reply to his
question.

"I'm Marcie," she gulped when she could speak again. "Marcie Locket. I live here with my parents."

Comet dipped his head in a bow. "I am honored to meet you, Marcie," he said politely.

"Um . . . me too," Marcie blurted out. She recalled something the pony had just said. "What's . . . the Lightning Herd?"

"We are a family of horses who live on Rainbow Mist Island," Comet told her proudly. "Our leader is wise and strong. He is called Blaze. A Stone of Power protects our herd from the dark horses who would like to steal our magic."

Marcie listened carefully, still having trouble taking all this in.

"So why are you *here*?" she asked him.

Comet gave a soft blow. "My twin sister,

Destiny, lost the Stone of Power when
we were cloud-racing. I found it and it
is safe again, but Destiny does not know
this. She thought she was in terrible
trouble for losing the stone, so she ran
away to hide in your world. I have come
here to look for her."

Marcie's curiosity seemed to be
getting the better of her shock. "You
and your twin sister were *cloud-racing*?
But how . . ."

Comet backed away from the fence.
"I will show you. Stay there," he neighed
gently.

Marcie felt a strange warm tingling
sensation flow to the very tips of her
fingers as violet sparkles bloomed in
Comet's dapple-gray coat and a veil of
shimmering rainbow mist surrounded him.

The gray pony disappeared and in its place stood a magnificent young cream-colored pony, with a flowing gold mane and tail. Springing from his shoulders were powerful wings, covered with gleaming golden feathers.

"Oh wow!" Marcie gasped, absolutely spellbound. The winged pony was the most beautiful thing she had ever seen. She caught her breath. "C–Comet?"

"Yes, Marcie. It is still me," Comet said in a deep musical whinny.

But before she could get used to the sight of Comet in his true form, there was a final swirl of glittering rainbow mist and Comet reappeared as a handsome dapple-gray Connemara pony.

"That's a really cool disguise! Can Destiny use her magic to disguise herself, too?" Marcie asked.

Comet nodded. "But that will not save her from the dark horses if they discover her. She is in danger. I need to find her and take her back to the safety of Rainbow Mist Island. Will you help me, Marcie?"

Marcie saw that Comet's deep-violet eyes were shadowed by worry for his sister and her heart melted. "Of course I will. Oh, just wait until I write to my best friend, Lara, about you."

Comet swished his dark gray tail. "I am sorry, but you can tell no one about me and what I have told you!"

Marcie was disappointed. She would have loved to share this amazing secret with Lara. It would have been very special, more than ever with Lara living so far away now.

"You must promise," Comet said, looking at her with his big eyes.

Marcie nodded slowly. If it would

help protect his twin sister from the dark horses until Comet could find her, she was prepared to agree. "I promise. No one's going to hear anything about you and Destiny from me."

"Thank you, Marcie."

Reaching forward, Comet gently

bumped his nose against Marcie's arm. She reached up to pat his satiny cheek.

"Marcie? Are you still down there?" called a voice. Marcie stiffened as she looked back at the big flowering bushes that screened the field from the house. She caught a glimpse of her mom's bright blue top through a small gap in the leaves.

"Mom's coming!" she gasped in panic.

Oh no! There wasn't time for her to hide Comet. Her mom was going to see her new magical pony friend at any second! What was she going to do?

Chapter
THREE

"There you are, sweetie," Mrs. Locket
said, slipping her arm round Marcie's
shoulder as she came and stood beside her
at the fence. "I thought I'd find you here,
staring at that rickety old shed we were going
to turn into a stable. I hope you're not too
upset about having to wait for your pony."

"Um . . . well, I am a b–bit disappointed,"
Marcie stammered. Why didn't her mom

say anything about the gorgeous dapple-gray pony that was standing in the field as large as life?! Instead, she was just looking back at her in concern—it was almost as if she couldn't see Comet.

Marcie continued on carefully. "I don't feel all that bad. It's not as if I'm never going to be able to have one, is it?" She was surprised to find that now Comet had arrived, she really was okay about having to wait for a pony of her own.

"Thanks for being so understanding, Marcie. Your dad's taken it quite hard," Mrs. Locket said. She sighed. "I just hope it won't be too long before he finds work again."

"It won't be. I've got a good feeling about it," Marcie said.

"I hope you're right." Her mom
smiled and reached out to ruffle Marcie's
shoulder-length brown hair. "Well—
dinner's almost ready. I'm just about to
serve it. Are you coming in?"

Marcie looked at Comet, who
was listening to the conversation, his
intelligent eyes twinkling. It was really

odd. But Mrs. Locket *still* didn't seem to have noticed him.

"Marcie?"

Marcie's head snapped back. "I'll be there in a minute."

"All right then." Her mom turned and went back to the house.

Marcie waited until she was out of sight behind the bushes before talking to Comet. "I don't get it. What just happened?"

"I used my magic so that only you can hear and see me," Comet told her.

"Really?" Marcie was delighted. "So you're invisible now? That's really cool." She had a sudden idea. "Why don't you live in this paddock? No one will know except me. There's lots of juicy grass to eat, rainwater in the trough, and the shed for shelter if it rains. And I'll come and see you whenever I can!"

Comet nodded. "This is a good place to stay while I am searching for Destiny."

"Then it's settled," Marcie said happily. "I'd better go now, or Mom and Dad will wonder what's taking me so long. I'll sneak out to see you later."

"Thank you, Marcie." Comet turned and walked a few steps, then bent his head and began cropping the grass with his strong young teeth.

After a final glance over her shoulder, Marcie hurried back to the house. There was a brand-new pony in her paddock after all! But never in her wildest dreams could she have imagined that it would be one as amazing and magical as Comet!

Marcie was almost too excited to eat, but she made herself take her time. She didn't want her mom and dad to think she had a stomachache and make her take a nap.

After they finished dinner, Marcie helped load the dishwasher and her mom insisted she do an hour of homework. Sighing, she went upstairs to do it all in double-quick time—she wanted to spend every minute possible with Comet!

When Marcie was sure her mom and dad were engrossed in watching the news on TV, she decided to risk sneaking out to see Comet. She grabbed an apple from the fruit bowl on the kitchen table and quickly chopped it up before disappearing into the garden.

The sun was setting and streaks of peach and salmon pink colored

the darkening sky. It was a beautiful
evening, and as Marcie jogged down
the garden to the paddock, her heart
began beating fast. She couldn't wait to
see the magic pony again. But he wasn't
standing in the paddock where she'd left
him.

"Comet!" she called.

There was no answer. No handsome
dapple-gray pony came galloping up the
field. The door of the big old shed hung

open. Maybe Comet was inside. Marcie went into the paddock to look.

But he wasn't in the shed, or behind it, or anywhere else.

Marcie's high spirits took a dent as she wondered whether Comet had changed his mind about staying in the paddock. Maybe he had grown tired of waiting for her and gone to find someone else to help him search for Destiny.

"Comet! Where are you?" she called again, starting to get worried.

There was a faint rustling sound from behind her.

"I am here, Marcie," Comet nickered, blowing warm breath into her hair.

Marcie spun round, a huge grin spreading across her face. He smelled wonderful—of grass and fresh air and something sweet that was his own magical scent. She threw her arms around his neck and pressed her cheek to its silky warmth.

"Oh, I'm so glad you came back!" she burst out. "I thought that maybe you'd left because you didn't like it here."

"I like it very much." Comet's violet eyes glowed with amusement. "I simply went to have a look around while I was waiting for you. There might have been traces of where Destiny has passed by."

Lowering her arms, Marcie stepped back. "What sort of traces?" she asked curiously.

"Wherever Destiny goes, she leaves a trail of softly glowing hoofprints that are invisible to most people in your world," Comet told her, twitching his ears.

"Really?" Marcie said, amazed. "Will I be able to see them?"

Comet nodded. "But only if you are riding me or I am very close to you."

Marcie knew he must be longing to find his twin sister, who was all alone and missing her family. "I should be able to come and help you look for Destiny tomorrow. We usually go shopping together early on Saturdays. Mom and Dad always take hours, and it can be really boring. I'll make an excuse to stay here," she decided.

Comet looked pleased. "Thank you, Marcie."

Marcie remembered the apple in her jeans pocket. "I brought something for you."

She took the slices out and offered

them to Comet on her flattened palm.
The magic pony stretched forward and she
felt his soft lips nuzzling her cautiously as
he picked up a piece of apple.

He started crunching and in a few
moments he had eaten the whole apple.
"That was delicious. I like your human
food."

"Wait until you try carrots and
peppermints!" Marcie smiled, feeling a

rush of affection for her amazing new friend. "See you in the morning then. Sweet dreams," she called to him as she went toward the gate.

Chapter FOUR

"Are you sure that you don't want to change your mind and come with us?" Marcie's dad asked the following morning as he picked up his car keys.

"Positive!" Marcie said firmly. "You know I hate food shopping. I thought I'd . . . um . . . send Lara a really long e-mail. I want to know how she's doing at her new school, what her new house is like, and if there are lots of good places to go out riding on Tramp."

"Good idea, sweetie. You and Lara can catch up on all the pony news, like you used to," her dad said. His face clouded. "I bet she'll be disappointed to hear that you won't be getting a new pony after all."

"Maybe at first, but she'll understand, like I do," Marcie said brightly. "Some things are better when you have to wait for them." *Especially when you already have a secret magic pony friend to keep you company!* she thought.

"I'm glad you're able to see things that way," her dad said, looking happier.

"See you later!" Marcie waved as their car drove away and she closed the front door.

She pulled on her riding boots, grabbed her hat, and made herself a promise to e-mail Lara as soon as she got back from helping Comet look for Destiny.

Comet saw her coming toward the paddock and gave a whinny of welcome. The morning sun made his dapple-gray coat look like polished metal.

"Hi, Comet! We've got the whole morning to search for Destiny. Are you ready?" she sang out.

Comet tossed his head with eagerness, his deep-violet eyes flashing. "Yes, Marcie, but I need to do one thing first."

Marcie felt a warm prickling sensation flowing down to her fingertips as bright violet sparks bloomed in Comet's dapple-gray coat. There was a crackling sound and a flash of rainbow light, which quickly faded to reveal Comet standing there fully tacked-up.

"Wow! That's incredible," Marcie exclaimed at Comet's cleverness. He was full of surprises.

Comet pawed the ground. "Climb onto my back, Marcie."

Marcie checked that all the straps were tightened and then mounted. As the magic pony broke into a trot down to the far end of the paddock, Marcie moved in time to his strides. They reached the barred gate that led straight into Willow Lane, and Marcie opened it and closed it behind them.

A few feet down the quiet winding lane, she turned Comet onto a track that led along the edge of a field and then to open farmland. Marcie and Lara had often ridden Tramp here. She knew all the best bridleways through the woods and which farmers allowed riders to cross their land.

"Let's go, Comet!" Marcie cried, nudging him on.

Comet snorted eagerly, pulling at his bit, and sprang forward into a gallop.

Marcie crouched low on his back, her hair blowing in the warm breeze. Excitement raced through her. Comet was thrilling to ride, so smooth and exciting, and his warm magic seemed to spread around her, so that however fast they went, she felt perfectly safe.

Comet almost flew along, his hooves barely brushing the grass. His head turned

left and right as his sharp eyes searched
for any sign that Destiny had come this
way.

"Hold tight!" he told Marcie as he
surged up a slope that led to the crest of
a hill. At the top he paused, his mane
and tail stirring in the breeze, and then
plunged down the other side toward some
woods.

Marcie caught her breath, almost
laughing aloud with joy. Happiness
filled her. She loved nothing better in
the whole world than riding on a bright
sunny day.

Comet checked his stride and slowed
as they entered the shade of the trees.

Bright green ferns bordered the bridle
path on both sides and grew thickly
among the trees. They were so tall that

a dog or a very small pony could have hidden beneath them. Marcie peered into the undergrowth as they pressed on, keeping a lookout, but there was no sign of Destiny.

After a thorough search, they emerged from the woods.

"I do not think she came this way," Comet said, scanning the shallow ridge ahead of them, which was dotted with grazing sheep.

Marcie spotted two small ponies tethered in a field to one side. "Look! Maybe Destiny is disguised as one of those!" she cried.

Comet nickered with renewed interest as he cantered over to investigate. But neither of the shaggy little ponies was Destiny. He trotted away sadly.

"I only hope that Destiny has found a safe hiding place," Comet whinnied. "The dark horses are always watching and waiting to steal our magic."

"We'll find her. I know we will. There are lots more places to search around here. I'll show you." Marcie patted his neck and then clicked her tongue encouragingly.

They rode on, taking a circular route that eventually brought them back through the woods.

"I think we'd better head home now,"
Marcie decided reluctantly. "Mom and
Dad will be back soon."

Comet nodded.

They retraced their steps, but skirted
the bottom of the hill. The track came
out further down Willow Lane. Facing
them, Marcie could see the stone
pillars that marked the large gateway of
Blackberry Farm, which had been empty
for ages.

She noticed that there were cars on the
farmhouse drive and a woman was putting
curtains up at an upstairs window. The
stable block had been freshly painted.

On impulse, she reined in Comet
and they stopped beside one of the stone
pillars, out of sight of the main house.

"It looks like new people have moved

in," she commented. "I wonder what they're like."

Just then, a large muscular brown horse burst out of an open stable door. Tossing its head, it laid back its ears and raced toward them.

Chapter
FIVE

"Quick, Comet! We have to stop that horse from getting out!" Marcie cried. "The busy main road runs along the bottom of Willow Lane!"

Comet stepped forward and stood sideways to block the gateway.

The brown horse snorted as it slowed to a halt a few feet away. Rolling its eyes, it reared up onto its back legs.

"Watch out! It's going to kick!" Marcie warned, steeling herself for a painful blow as the horse's flailing hooves came within inches of hitting her leg. Though she was more scared that Comet would be hurt.

Pushing down on the stirrups, she stood up and waved her arms at the frightened horse, hoping it would turn aside and not try to bite or kick them.

Comet stood his ground. He turned his head to look at the brown horse and Marcie felt another tingling sensation flow down her fingers as violet sparks glowed in Comet's dapple-gray coat. A shimmering mist briefly surrounded the horse and then gradually faded along with every last violet spark.

The brown horse stood there, calm now. Its dark eyes were soft and kind. Comet gave a friendly blow and reached out to touch noses gently with it.

"Good job, Comet!" Marcie dismounted and moved slowly toward the loose horse. Luckily it wore a head collar, so she reached up and grasped hold. "Don't be scared. It's okay, I won't hurt you," she said reassuringly.

To her relief, it didn't throw up its head or try to back away.

"You were very brave to try to stop that horse," Comet said to Marcie.

"I didn't really think about it. I couldn't bear the idea of you being hurt. Anyway, you were brave, too," she said, looking at Comet adoringly. "I think we saved each other!"

"Oh, thank goodness. You've caught her!"

A boy, who looked about twelve years old, was running up to Marcie and Comet. He had fair hair that flopped forward onto his forehead and an open, friendly face.

A younger girl came pounding after him. The girl caught up to the boy and stood there, breathing hard.

"What's happening? Is Drift all
right?" she demanded, frowning.

The boy looked at her. "She's fine.
Don't panic, Sally. Luckily, this girl
caught her before she hurt herself." He
took a lead rope out of his jeans pocket
and clipped it on to the brown horse's
head collar.

"And we're fine, too, thanks," Marcie

said drily. It had been pretty scary to have Drift run straight at her and Comet.

"Oh yeah. Sorry about that. Drift's a total sweetie, except when she's having one of her off days!" he said to Marcie with a narrow grin.

"Like today?" Marcie guessed, smiling. "I'm Marcie Locket. I live just up the road."

"Hi, Marcie. I'm Ian Bale and this girl, who looks like she's just sucked a lemon, is my sister, Sally."

"Very funny. Not!" Sally shot back at him.

She also had fair hair, held back from her face by a brown velvet headband, and there was a sprinkle of freckles on her cheeks. She looked about nine years old and would have been very pretty if she hadn't been scowling fiercely.

"You total idiot, Ian. You should have kept your eye on Drift," Sally scolded her brother. "You know what she can be like. Here, I'll take her."

"Me? *You* left the stable door open!" Ian said.

"I did not!" Sally's cheeks flamed.

"Yes, you di—Oh, forget it," Ian said, shrugging. He obviously couldn't be bothered to get into an argument in front of Marcie and Comet. Sighing, he handed Sally the leading rope. "Suit yourself."

His sister flashed him a triumphant grin and then clicked her tongue at Drift. Turning on her heel, she led the horse back toward the stables.

"Oh, by the way, thanks," Sally murmured, not bothering to look back at Marcie.

"No problem," Marcie called after her.

Ian flashed Marcie a wry grin. "Don't mind Sally. She's a drama queen, but she never stays grumpy for long." He ran an appreciative eye over Comet. "He's a Connemara, isn't he? They're good all-rounders, aren't they? We used to have one. What's he called?"

"Comet," Marcie told him.

"Hello, boy." Ian put up his hand so Comet could nuzzle it. "How long have

you had him?" he asked Marcie.

"Not very long. Actually he's . . . um
. . . on loan," Marcie said vaguely, hoping
to avoid awkward questions. "I didn't know
that anyone had moved into Blackberry
Farm. How long have you been here?" she
asked, quickly changing the subject.

"Just a couple of weeks," Ian told her.
"I really like it here. It seems like there'll
be lots of good places to ride."

"There are," Marcie agreed. "I could
show you and Sally some, if you like. Do
you have any other horses or ponies besides
Drift?"

"Yeah, we've got Rufus and Fiddler, too.
Would you like to come and meet them?"

"I'd love to—" Marcie began, but then
she remembered that she was supposed to be
hurrying home before her parents returned

from shopping. "I can't now, though. I have to get back home."

"No problem," Ian said easily. "Why don't you come over tomorrow? Sally and I plan to go riding—if she's in a better mood, that is. You and Comet could come, too, and you can show us around."

"Sounds great," Marcie said, beaming. It would give her and Comet another chance to search for Destiny.

They arranged a time to meet up and then Marcie remounted Comet. "Bye!" She waved to Ian before they rode up the lane.

"Ian was really nice, wasn't he?" Marcie said, once they were out of earshot.

Comet nodded. "I like him, too."

"I'm not so sure about Sally, though," Marcie commented. "She seemed a bit grumpy. I hope Ian's right when he says she's usually okay. I'm looking forward to going riding with them tomorrow."

Comet's deep-violet eyes glowed under his long eyelashes. Marcie knew he was hoping he'd find Destiny.

Back home, she turned Comet out into the paddock. There was a small fountain of violet sparkles as the tack disappeared. Comet shook himself and then walked over to the trough for a long drink.

Marcie smiled at him. "I'll come out to see you later and bring you some carrots," she promised.

Inside the house, she quickly checked that her mom and dad weren't home and then dumped her riding boots and hat in the utility room. After grabbing a cold drink, she went and sat at the family computer to write to Lara. She wished she could tell her all about the magical time she had been having with Comet!

Marcie was halfway through her e-mail when she heard a car door slam. She looked out the window to see her dad coming up the drive carrying bags of groceries.

The front door opened and then he stuck his head round the sitting-room door. "Are you still on that computer, young lady? You must have an awful lot to tell Lara!" he teased.

Marcie beamed at him. "I do!" *If only you knew*, she thought. "Guess what? I just met the two kids who moved into Blackberry Farm: Sally and Ian Bale," she told him, her enthusiasm running away with her. "And they've got a horse and two ponies! I've got some new horsey friends and they live just down the road!"

Mr. Locket looked puzzled. "Really? Well, that is a bit of good luck, especially now that Lara isn't here. But how come you met Ian and Sally? I thought you said you'd be staying in the house. You know the rules about always letting us know where you are when you go out," he said sternly.

Marcie realized her mistake. She thought fast. She could hardly tell her dad that she'd been perfectly safe because she was with Comet. "Um . . . no, I didn't exactly go anywhere," she lied. "They . . . uh . . . came past on their ponies and I just went outside onto the driveway to talk to them. In fact, they asked me to go riding with them tomorrow!"

Chapter
SIX

Marcie woke early the following morning to find sunshine streaming through a gap in the curtains.

"Yay! I'm going riding again on Comet!" she said to herself as she leaped out of bed and quickly dressed in jeans and a T-shirt.

Her dad was already downstairs when Marcie appeared. The delicious smell of frying bacon met her as she opened the kitchen door.

"Dad! You're up early," Marcie said, surprised. He usually liked to sleep in on Sundays.

He smiled, looking a bit weary. "I didn't sleep very well with so much on my mind. So I thought I'd make breakfast. Bacon-and-egg sandwiches are on the menu, if you're interested."

"You bet! Can I cut the bread?" Marcie asked helpfully.

"Thanks, sweetie. You must be looking forward to meeting up with your new friends. It's nice of them to invite you riding with them," he commented.

"Yes, it is." Marcie flipped her hair over her shoulder as she wielded the bread knife. The slices were a bit uneven, but

her dad didn't seem to notice.

As soon as she'd finished breakfast,
Marcie put on her riding gear and then
said good-bye to her parents. "See you
later! I'll take the shortcut across the
paddock."

She felt a thrill of excitement when she
saw Comet standing with his head over the
fence waiting for her. As she approached
him, Comet curled his dark gray lips and
greeted her with a neigh of welcome. He
was already tacked-up and eager to go.

Marcie swung herself into the saddle and leaned over to pat his silky neck as they set off.

Ian and Sally were waiting for them in the stable yard. Ian was on a handsome chestnut pony with two white socks. Marcie guessed that this was Rufus. He waved as she and Comet rode through the front gates.

"Hi, Marcie!" Sally waved, too. She was just mounting a pretty palomino.

"What a lovely pony!" Marcie said, pleased to see that Sally seemed in a better mood today.

Sally smiled, her blue eyes sparkling. "Thanks. Fiddler's really sweet."

"We usually take turns exercising the ponies," Ian told her, controlling Rufus as the chestnut pony sidestepped.

"Poor old Drift doesn't look too happy at being left behind."

Marcie glanced to where the big brown horse was standing with her head over the paddock fence, watching them with mournful dark eyes. As Ian and Sally rode out on to Willow Lane in single file, Marcie gave Drift one last sympathetic look before following behind the others.

"I thought we could ride up to the old water tower on the hill. The view is great from up there," Marcie said. It was also in the opposite direction to where she and Comet had already searched, which meant they would be able to explore a different area.

"I hope we'll find Destiny this time or some sign that she came this way," she whispered to him as they reached the main road and waited at the crossing.

"I hope so, too!" Comet replied.

Marcie froze, surprised that he had spoken aloud to her with Ian and Sally so close. But neither of them seemed to have noticed anything odd.

"Do not worry, Marcie," Comet told her, as if he knew what she was thinking. "Only you can hear me speaking.

Everyone else will just think I am neighing or snorting."

"Cool!" Marcie whispered in reply, relaxing.

Once safely across the main road, Marcie took a side turn and led the way down a wide, grassy track lined with hedges. The hawthorn was still covered with clusters of creamy flowers. Their sweet, musty scent filled the air.

After a few miles the track opened out onto a sweep of hillside covered with sparse-looking grass. Marcie squeezed Comet into a gallop and Ian and Sally did the same. Rabbits dived for cover as the ponies sped past.

Ahead of them the ground rose steeply to where an old stone building topped the hill.

"Race you to the top!" Sally cried, crouching low on Fiddler.

"You're on! Whoo-hoo!" Ian yelled, urging Rufus forward.

Comet couldn't resist. He shot after the ponies in a lightning burst of speed. In a thunder of hooves, he streaked past them, his dark gray tail flying out behind him like a silken banner.

"Yay! Eat our dust!" Marcie yelled over her shoulder.

Rufus and Fiddler stretched out and
gave chase, but they couldn't match
Comet's powerful stride. Marcie thought
she noticed the shadow of a large horse
spreading across the hillside as Comet
raced past, but then it was gone, so she
must have imagined it. They reached
the top of the hill, twenty feet ahead of
the others. She reined Comet in beside
the water tower and they stood waiting
for Ian and Sally.

"What kept you?" Marcie joked as
they rode up.

Ian laughed. "I thought Rufus was
fast, but Comet can *really* move!" he said
admiringly.

"That was fun!" Sally said, her face
glowing.

They sat in a line looking out at the

view over the green rolling hills. In the distance they could see a gray smudge where the hills met the sky.

Marcie wondered where Destiny could be hiding in this wide-open space, broken only by isolated farms and the occasional cow shed or barn.

They continued on, riding more slowly and enjoying the fresh air and sunshine. In the fold of two hills, there was a fast-running stream and they stopped to let the ponies drink.

Marcie bent close to whisper to Comet. "I haven't seen any signs that Destiny's been this way? Have you?"

Comet shook his head, twitching one ear disappointedly. "Not yet."

An hour later, Ian announced that he

was hungry and suggested they go back to Blackberry Farm for lunch. And with rumbling tummies, everyone agreed.

Back at the farm, Ian and Sally untacked their ponies. Drift lifted her head and nickered a welcome from the paddock, seemingly very pleased not to be by herself any longer. As the ponies all seemed to be getting along well together, Ian suggested that Marcie turn out Comet with them.

Mrs. Bale made an enormous and hearty lunch, which they ate at a big wooden table in the farmhouse kitchen. Salad and baked potatoes with cheese, followed by homemade vanilla cupcakes with chocolate frosting, all washed down with lemonade. After lunch, Sally took Marcie up to her bedroom and excitedly showed her all the ribbons and trophies she'd won on Fiddler. Marcie found herself having the best time she'd had since Lara had lived in her town. She would have liked to stay longer, but thought she'd better check that Comet was still happy at being left in the Bales' paddock with the other ponies.

Sally walked out to the stable yard with her. "I had a great time today," she said, a smile lighting up her pretty face.

"Me too," Marcie said. "Thanks for showing me your trophies and stuff."

"Of course. I just got a great new book about braiding manes and tails. You can borrow it sometime, if you'd like."

"That sounds cool. Thanks," Marcie said warmly, pleased that she and Sally were now getting along so well. Maybe she'd ask her to come over soon and they could watch her favorite movie, *Black Beauty*.

Ian was in the tack room, hanging up clean bridles and folding horse blankets. "I'll do this all by myself, then, huh?" he teased, rolling his eyes at his sister.

"Yeah! Why don't you?" Sally gave him a playful shove, but began helping him.

Marcie grinned. Those two were a double act! Shaking her head slowly, she walked the few feet to the paddock.

"Are you ready to go home now?" she whispered to Comet.

"Yes. I thought I might go out searching for Destiny again," Comet told her. "But I do not think you should come with me, as I sensed the dark horses' presence earlier."

Marcie felt a prickle of concern. So she hadn't been imagining things—that dark shadow was real. Would Comet's magic be strong enough to protect him from his enemies when he was so far from home?

Her mind was filled by this worrying thought as she led him out and let the paddock gate shut itself behind her with a soft click.

Chapter
SEVEN

As it was getting dark, Marcie slipped
into the garden to check that Comet had
returned after his latest search.

To her relief he was there, his gray
coat gleaming softly in the moonlight.
Her heart swelled with happiness and
pride as she looked at him. She didn't
think she'd ever get over the incredible
feeling of being friends with a magic pony.

"Greetings, Marcie," Comet snorted softly.

"I was worried about you," she admitted. "What would happen if the dark horses found you while you were looking for Destiny?" she asked him.

"Before I came here I looked into the Stone of Power to see where Destiny was. Its magic still gives me some protection," he told her.

Reassured, Marcie gave him some pieces of carrot from her pocket. Comet crunched them up eagerly. She spent a few more minutes with him, saying good night, and then hurried back indoors before her parents noticed she was gone.

Mr. Locket had just finished using the computer.

Marcie asked if she could use it and e-mailed Lara to tell her about her ride with Ian and Sally. She didn't mention Comet, but said that she'd borrowed Drift to ride. She sent the message, and after a couple of minutes, Lara e-mailed back to say that she'd love to meet Ian, Sally, and their ponies when she came to visit. Marcie signed out and then logged off. She was feeling happier than she had for some time as she went upstairs to read for a while before going to bed. But she had only just opened her book, when she heard a loud knock on the front door.

She sat up, frowning. Who could it be this late?

Marcie came out of her bedroom as her dad answered the door.

Ian's panicky voice floated up to her. "Is Marcie there? All the ponies have escaped! Can she come and help us look for them?"

"Oh no!" Marcie ran down the stairs. "What happened? How did they get out?" Ian avoided her eyes.

"Um . . . it doesn't really matter. Sally's already out looking for them with Mom and Dad. I came to ask you to help because you know the area better than we do."

"I'll go grab a flashlight!" Marcie turned to her mom and dad. "It's okay if I go, isn't it?"

They nodded. "Of course you should help, but you can't go out in the middle of the night by yourself," her dad said.

"We'll come, too," her mom decided.

After grabbing coats, boots, and flashlights, Marcie, Ian, and her mom and dad set out. They walked around the road and turned into the top of Willow Lane. Sally and her mom came hurrying up to them.

"Any sign of the ponies?" Ian asked his sister.

In the dim light Sally's face looked pale and drawn. She shook her head. "Dad thinks they might have cut across the fields opposite ours. He went to look." Her voice

broke into a sob. "Oh, I hope they did. I can't bear to think about them getting out on to the main road . . ."

Marcie went to put a comforting hand on Sally's arm.

But Sally twisted away distractedly. "Don't touch me!" she snapped.

Marcie tried not to feel hurt. Sally must have been so upset that she hardly knew what she was saying. Marcie didn't blame her. She knew she'd be crazy with worry if anything happened to Comet.

Comet! He would find the missing ponies in no time, but how could she get away from the others and go to ask him for his help?

"I'll . . . um . . . check on this side," Marcie decided on impulse. "Dad? Why don't you and Mom get the car and meet me down at the other field. The one with the gate that leads out to the main road."

"It makes sense to split up," her mom agreed. "And Marcie knows these fields like the back of her hand." She turned to Marcie. "Don't take any risks, sweetie. If you see any sign of the ponies, stand still and keep turning your flashlight on and off until someone comes to help you."

"I will," Marcie promised, already

pointing the flashlight to illuminate her way as she walked over the cattle guard into the first field.

She crossed her fingers, hoping that none of the others would follow. Luckily, Ian went off with Sally and their mom, while Marcie's parents headed for their garage. Marcie was about to head back toward Comet's paddock, when her fingers began to tingle and Comet himself appeared beside her in a cloud of shimmering rainbow mist.

"Comet! What are you doing here? I was just about to come and look for you!"

"I heard all the voices and guessed what had happened. Hurry! Climb on my back, Marcie! Do not worry. I have used my magic to make you invisible too when you are riding me."

Marcie mounted. She twisted her hands into his dark gray mane and held on tight.

"I'm ready!"

Comet sped away, moving as fast as the wind. A protective bubble of rainbow sparkles surrounded Marcie, keeping her safe on top of Comet's back. One. Two. Three. The fields rushed past in a magical

blur. There was no sign of the ponies.

Down in the field, Comet raced alongside the tall hedges toward the gate. They had to find the ponies before they reached it and were spooked by the traffic in the road beyond. Comet sped on, his flashing hooves eating up the ground.

Suddenly, Marcie spotted three shadowy fast-moving shapes in the distance.

"Look there's Drift, Rufus, and Fiddler!" she gasped. "Thank goodness they're all together."

"I see them, too," Comet neighed.

Leaping forward in another dizzying burst of speed, he easily closed the distance between them. Comet rode up alongside the terrified ponies. Marcie's fingers tingled again as he sent out an invisible spray of violet sparks that settled on them like soft rain.

The runaway ponies gradually slowed to a trot and then a walking pace. Finally they stopped, their sides heaving.

Marcie was still worried. Any one of the ponies could get scared by a sudden noise and bolt again. And the gate to the main road was horribly close.

"Do you think you could use your magic to make them follow you?" she asked urgently.

Comet nodded. "I have an idea. This way they will get to safety more quickly."

There was another violet flash of Comet's sparkly magic, and rainbow shimmers whirled around them all. Marcie felt the air whistle past her ears as

they all found themselves flying through
the night with the stars twinkling above
them. There was a slight jolt as Comet's
hooves touched down further up the field.
The other ponies were safely beside him.

"Wow! You were amazing, Comet!"
Marcie said, dismounting.

"I am glad I could help."

She was reaching up to hug him, when
she felt him stiffen and lean down to stare
at the grass.

Marcie looked down, too. In front of them both and stretching away up the hill was a faint line of softly glowing violet hoofprints.

"Destiny! She came this way!" Comet whinnied excitedly.

Marcie felt a pang. Did that mean that he was leaving, right now? "Are . . . are you going after her?" she asked anxiously.

Comet shook his head. "No. The trail is cold. But it proves Destiny was here," he said, his eyes glowing with fresh hope. "When she is very close, I will be able to hear her hoofbeats. And then I may have to leave suddenly, without saying good-bye."

Marcie bit her lip as she realized she had secretly been hoping that he might stay forever. "Couldn't you and

Destiny live here with me and share your
paddock?" she asked hopefully.

"No, Marcie, that is not possible. We
must return to our family on Rainbow
Mist Island," Comet explained gently.

Marcie swallowed hard, feeling
tears well up. "I guess I knew that," she
admitted. She forced herself to smile as she
decided not to think about Comet leaving
and to enjoy every moment with him.

Just then a car swung off the main road and pulled into the gateway. Its headlights streamed into the field onto Marcie, Comet, and the ponies. Marcie felt herself tense and then relax again as she remembered that Comet was invisible to everyone except her.

"I am not needed now. I will see you tomorrow, Marcie." Comet disappeared in a final shower of violet sparkles that glistened as they fell around Marcie's feet.

"Marcie! You found them!" Her mom and dad had opened the gate and were walking toward her. Moments later, Ian, Sally, and Mr. and Mrs. Bale appeared at the top of the field, their flashlights wobbling as they came running toward the Lockets from the opposite direction.

"There they are! It's our ponies!"

Sally cried, dashing forward.

Fiddler nickered softly as she saw her.
Sally flung her arms round the palomino's
neck and burst into tears of relief.

"It's okay, Sally. Fiddler isn't injured.
They're all fine," Marcie said reassuringly.
She wished she could have told Sally
about how amazing Comet had been,
but of course, she never would.

Sally turned to Marcie, her face twisted in anger. "No thanks to you! It was your fault in the first place! You left the paddock gate unlatched. That's why the ponies escaped!"

Chapter
EIGHT

Marcie blinked at Sally in shock and dismay.

"I . . . I didn't. I closed the paddock gate after I let Com—" she began and broke off in confusion, as she remembered that she couldn't mention the magic pony in front of her parents. They had no idea that he even existed.

Sally's lip curled. "You obviously didn't bother to check if it was closed properly.

Don't try and get out of this. You could at least say sorry!"

"I would apologize, but I honestly don't think I left the gate open," Marcie said reasonably.

But Sally was too wound up to listen. "I don't believe you! Stay away from me. I don't want to talk to you!" she shouted. She whirled around and stomped away.

Marcie watched her go, speechless. "Ian. You believe me, don't you?" She turned to him, hoping that he would listen to her.

But he shrugged and looked very embarrassed. "I . . . I don't know, Marcie. Leave it for now. You can't get through to Sally when she's like this," he said. He turned to his dad. "Let's get the ponies home."

Mr. Bale nodded. He thanked
Marcie's mom and dad for helping to
search for the ponies.

Mrs. Bale turned to Marcie.
"Whatever did happen, no harm's done.
Don't worry about it now. Let's all go
home," she suggested.

"Everything will seem clearer after a
good night's sleep," Mrs. Locket agreed.
"Come on, Marcie. We'll all drive back."

Marcie's heart was heavy as she trudged through the gate and went toward the car with her parents. "I don't get it. Why is everyone blaming me?" she gulped, close to tears.

"They're tired and upset," her dad soothed. "I suggest you go see Ian and Sally when they've had a chance to calm down."

"It won't do any good. I know what Sally's like. She hates me now," Marcie said miserably.

Their promising new friendship looked like it was over before it had even begun.

Over the next few days, Marcie racked her brain, trying to remember whether she had left the Bales' paddock gate open.

She was talking to Comet one
morning before she left for school. "I
remember that I was worried about
you meeting those horrible dark horses
when I let you out of the Bales' paddock.
Maybe I wasn't concentrating and I left
the gate off the latch. If I'm honest, I'm
not even sure anymore."

Comet's deep-violet eyes softened.
"Even if you did, it was not done
deliberately."

"Try telling Sally that," Marcie said
sadly. "I've gone over twice after school
and called, but she won't even talk to me.
She's my best friend here now that Lara's
moved away. No one at school loves
ponies as much as we do! Even Ian's only
just about speaking to me, and I'm sure
he's just being polite. I know he secretly

blames me for letting the ponies escape. I feel awful!"

Comet leaned toward her and huffed out a soft warm breath. "You are a kind person and good friend."

Marcie felt herself calming down as she stroked his velvety dark-gray muzzle.

"Thanks for believing in me. You're the best friend anyone could have," she said fondly.

Comet fell silent and his ears swiveled thoughtfully.

"What?" Marcie asked.

"Do you remember the day we met Ian and Sally at the farm gateway?"

Marcie nodded. How could she forget? "You stopped Drift from hurting us and galloping out into Willow Lane, didn't you? Sally and Ian were arguing about who'd left the stable door open."

"That is right." Comet's mane stirred in the breeze. "Did they not also say that Drift could be difficult?"

"Yes," Marcie agreed, trying to remember exactly what the Bales had said about the big brown horse. "I got the impression that she likes escaping and running off."

"That is what I thought." Comet

snorted in satisfaction, his eyes twinkling mysteriously.

Marcie frowned, still puzzled. What was Comet getting at?

"I think you should go and see Ian and Sally again," Comet decided, swishing his tail.

"Really? I'm not sure it would do any good," Marcie said doubtfully, but she trusted Comet's judgment. "I will, if you think I should."

Comet nodded. "I do, Marcie. Friendship is important. Is it not worth fighting for?"

"I guess it is," Marcie agreed. "I'll give it one more try, and this time I'm not leaving until Sally agrees to talk to me. We'll go over to Blackberry Farm as soon as I get home after school. Okay?"

Comet nodded, his eyes shining with wisdom.

Marcie was so nervous about their plan to go and see Sally and Ian that she could hardly concentrate in class.

Somehow she managed to get through her schoolwork. Luckily, they were working on their projects. Marcie's was about heavy horses and their lives, so she found herself enjoying writing a page about shire horses. It was a surprise when the bell rang for the end of class and she could rush out to meet her mom.

"You seem a bit more cheerful," Mrs. Locket said as she parked the car in their driveway. "Did you make up with Ian and Sally?"

"Not yet. But I'm working on it!"

She changed out of her school clothes
and was about to go out to Comet when
the house phone rang.

Her mom picked it up.

Marcie heard her say, "When did
this happen?" *It's your dad*, Mrs. Locket
mouthed at her silently.

Marcie crossed her fingers and toes
for good luck as she waited for her mom
to put the phone down. *Please, please let it
be good news*, she prayed. Mrs. Locket took
a deep breath and stood with her hand on
her chest. Marcie almost exploded with
impatience.

"Mo-om! What's going on?"

"I can hardly believe it myself," her
mom said, blinking dazedly. "Your dad's
just been offered a new job, much better
than his last one. He starts next week.

It pays a lot more than he's been getting. So I think you can start looking at ponies for sale!"

"Really? Yay! That's amazing! Good for Dad!" Marcie squealed. She grabbed her mom and they did a triumphant little dance up and down the hall.

She was going to get her pony and Comet would have a new friend to share the paddock with! She couldn't wait to e-mail Lara and tell her the fabulous news, not mentioning Comet, of course. But first, she was going to Blackberry Farm.

"I'm going to make Sally see what she's missing by not being my friend," she told her mom determinedly.

"Good for you, sweetie. That's the way. It might be tough to get her to talk to you, though. Do you want me to come with you?"

"No. I have to do this on my own," Marcie said firmly, already halfway out of the door. "I won't be long."

At the paddock, she told Comet the good news about her dad's new job.

His intelligent eyes shone. "That is

wonderful, Marcie. What sort of pony would you like?"

"A Connemara, of course! What else?" Marcie said immediately. "Everything's getting better now. It would be just perfect if Ian and Sally wanted to be friends with me again."

Comet didn't reply. He tossed his head, and in a flash and a cloud of violet sparkles he was fully tacked-up. "Climb on my back, Marcie!" he neighed.

As they rode out on to Willow Lane, Marcie's bright self-confidence wavered. What if Sally still wasn't prepared to listen to her?

They had reached the curve in the road, just before Blackberry Farm, when Marcie heard a sound she had been longing for and dreading at the same time.

The hollow sound of hooves galloping overhead.

"Destiny!" Comet veered off into the nearby field, following the magical hoofbeats, which sounded louder and closer. Panting with excitement, he halted briefly beside a hedge.

"You must get down now, Marcie," he told her gently. Marcie dismounted. She knew that this time he was leaving. Her heart ached with sadness, but she knew she would have to be very strong.

There was a violet flash and a twinkling rainbow mist floated down around Comet. He stood there in his true form, a dapple-gray pony no longer, but a magnificent magic pony with a noble head, cream coat, and spreading golden wings. His golden mane and tail flowed down in shimmering silken strands.

"Comet!" Marcie gasped. She had almost forgotten how beautiful he was.

"I hope you catch Destiny. Good luck! I'll never forget you!" she said, her voice breaking.

Comet's deep-violet eyes clouded over for a moment with sadness. "Farewell, young friend. Ride well and true," he said in a deep musical voice.

There was a final violet flash of light and a silent burst of rainbow sparkles that showered down around Marcie in crystal droplets and tinkled as they hit the grass.

Comet spread his wings and soared upward. He faded and was gone.

Marcie gulped back tears, hardly able to believe that this had happened so fast. Something glittered on the grass. It was a single shimmering gold wing-feather. Reaching down, she picked it up. It tingled against her palm as it faded to a cream color. She slipped it into her pocket, knowing that she would treasure it always as a reminder of the wonderful adventure she had shared with the magic pony.

As Marcie stepped back out onto Willow Lane, Sally waved at her from the farm gate.

"Marcie! Come here," she cried. "I have something to show you!"

Quickly wiping her eyes, Marcie followed. Sally didn't seem to be quite as angry with her right now. Marcie was puzzled.

Ian was standing by the stable door, just out of sight of Fiddler, Rufus, and Drift in the nearby paddock. He gestured to Marcie to be quiet. "Watch this," he whispered, pointing at Drift.

The brown horse pricked her ears. She walked up to the gate. Leaning her weight against the catch, Drift used her teeth to spring it, so that the gate swung slowly open. Ian quickly rushed forward, closed it again and slipped a loop of rope over it, before she could escape.

Marcie blinked in astonishment. "So that's how all the ponies got out!"

"Yes. It was Drift. She can open doors and gates. I'm so sorry that I blamed you. I've been so mean, haven't I?" Sally said.

Marcie realized that Comet had worked all this out. This was his final gift to her before he had to leave forever.

"Who cares?" Grinning widely, she gave Sally a big hug. "I'm just glad we can be friends again!"

You were right, Comet! Marcie said silently. *Friendship is worth fighting for.* Wherever he was, she knew that his

deep-violet eyes would be shining with
approval.

Don't miss

Magic Ponies: A New Friend

Coming soon

Magic Ponies: A Twinkle of Hooves

Magic Ponies: Show-Jumping Dreams

Don't miss these
Magic Kitten books!

Don't miss these
Magic Puppy books!

About the AUTHOR

Sue Bentley's books for children often include animals, fairies, and wildlife. She lives in Northampton, England, and enjoys reading, going to the movies, and watching the birds on the feeders outside her window. She loves horses, which she thinks are all completely magical. One of her favorite books is *Black Beauty*, which she must have read at least ten times. At school she was always getting scolded for daydreaming, but she now knows that she was storing up ideas for when she became a writer. Sue has met and owned many animals, but the wild creatures in her life hold a special place in her heart.